good morning, neighbor

DAVIDE CALI
MARIA DEK

PRINCETON ARCHITECTURAL PRESS · NEW YORK

A MOUSE wanted to make an omelet.
To make an omelet the mouse needed an egg,
but he didn't have one.

So he thought,
"I'll go and ask my neighbor,
the BLACKBIRD."

"GOOD MORNING, NEIGHBOR.
Do you have an egg that I could use
to make an omelet?"

"I'm sorry, I don't,"
said the blackbird.
"But I do have *flour*. With an
egg we could make a cake!
Let's go and ask my neighbor,
the DORMOUSE."

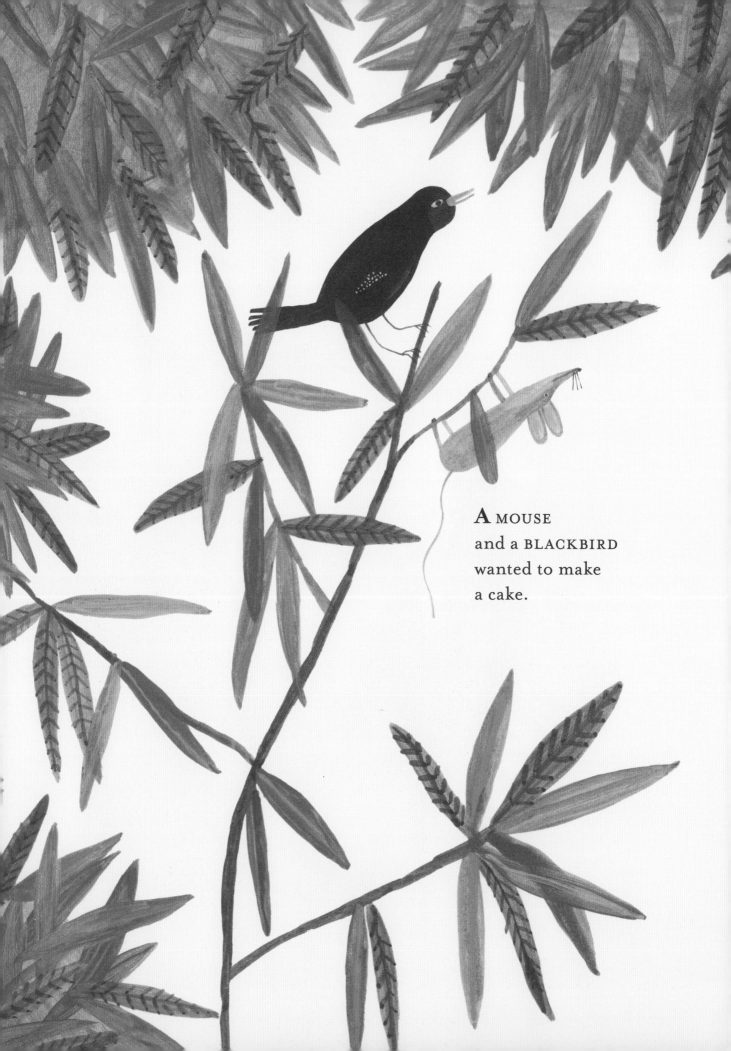

A MOUSE
and a BLACKBIRD
wanted to make
a cake.

"GOOD MORNING, NEIGHBOR.
Do you have an egg that we could use
to make a cake?"

"I'm sorry, I don't," said the dormouse.
"But I do have *butter.*
You'll need butter to make a cake.
For the egg we can ask
my neighbor, the MOLE."

A MOUSE,
a BLACKBIRD,
and a DORMOUSE
wanted to make
a cake.

"GOOD MORNING, NEIGHBOR.
Do you have an egg that we could use
to make a cake?"

"I'm sorry, I don't,"
said the mole. "But I do have *sugar*.
You'll definitely need sugar
to make a cake!" Perhaps
my neighbor, the HEDGEHOG,
will loan us an egg."

A MOUSE,
a BLACKBIRD,
a DORMOUSE,
and a MOLE
wanted to make
a cake.

"GOOD MORNING, NEIGHBOR.
Do you have an egg that we could use
to make a cake?"

"**I'm sorry, I don't,**" said the hedgehog.
"What kind of cake do you want
to make? I have *apples*, maybe we can
make an apple cake. My neighbor,
the RACCOON, might have an egg."

A MOUSE, a BLACKBIRD,
a DORMOUSE, a MOLE,
and a HEDGEHOG
wanted to make
a cake.

"GOOD MORNING, NEIGHBOR.
Do you have an egg that we could use
to make a cake?"

"I'm sorry, I don't," said the raccoon.
"But I have *cinnamon* to add flavor.
Let's go see if my neighbor,
the LIZARD, has an egg."

A MOUSE,
a BLACKBIRD,
a DORMOUSE,
a MOLE,
a HEDGEHOG,
and a RACCOON
wanted to make
a cake.

"GOOD MORNING, NEIGHBOR.
Do you have an egg that we could use
to make a cake?"

"I'm sorry, I don't," said the lizard.
"But I do have *raisins!*
For the egg we can ask my neighbor,
the BAT."

A MOUSE,
a BLACKBIRD,
a DORMOUSE,
a MOLE,
a HEDGEHOG,
a RACCOON,
and a LIZARD
wanted to make
a cake.

They already had flour,
butter, sugar, apples,
cinnamon, and raisins.

The only thing
missing was the egg.

"Of course I have an egg!"
said the bat.
The neighbors finally had
all the ingredients they needed.

And so they began.

The BLACKBIRD poured the *flour*.
The BAT broke the *egg*.
The DORMOUSE added the *butter*,
and the MOLE stirred in the *sugar*.
The MOUSE mixed the dough.
Then the HEDGEHOG added the *apples*,
the RACCOON sprinkled the *cinnamon*,
and the LIZARD topped it with *raisins*.

"**All we need now is an oven.**
Let's ask our neighbor, the OWL,"
said the lizard.

A MOUSE,
a BLACKBIRD,
a DORMOUSE,
a MOLE,
a HEDGEHOG,
a RACCOON,
a LIZARD,
and a BAT
wanted to make
a cake.

The cake was ready to be baked.
All they needed was an oven.

"GOOD MORNING, NEIGHBOR.
Could we use your oven to bake a cake?"

"Certainly," said the owl.
So all of the animals joined
the owl in her kitchen.

The cake finally came out of the oven, and it was perfect.
But when it was time to serve it, the owl asked,

"How many slices should I cut?"

The BLACKBIRD put in the *flour,*
so she gets a slice.

The DORMOUSE put in the *butter,*
so he gets a slice.

The MOLE offered the *sugar,*
so obviously she gets a slice.

The HEDGEHOG provided the *apples,*
so he gets a slice too.

A slice also goes to the RACCOON
for adding the *cinnamon.*

And a slice goes to the LIZARD
for pitching in the *raisins.*

Lastly, a slice goes to the BAT
for putting in the *egg.*

And we must not forget
a slice for the OWL,
for the use of her *oven.*

So that makes 8 slices in all.

"What about me?" asked the mouse.

"You didn't put in anything,"
said the dormouse.
"So you don't get a slice.
And, anyway, it's hard to cut
a cake into 9 slices."

The mouse went away sadly while
the other animals began to divide the cake.

"**Well,**" said the BLACKBIRD,
"if the mouse hadn't asked me for an egg,
I wouldn't have thought about giving him
flour to make the cake."

"**And if he hadn't asked me for an egg,**
I wouldn't have put in the *butter*,"
said the DORMOUSE.

"And I wouldn't have offered the *sugar*,"
said the MOLE.

"And I wouldn't have pitched in the *apples*,"
said the HEDGEHOG.

"And I wouldn't have added the *cinnamon*,"
said the RACCOON.

"And I wouldn't have pitched in the *raisins*,"
said the LIZARD.

"And we wouldn't have a *cake* to share,"
said the BAT.

"You're right!"
said the OWL.

And so the BLACKBIRD,
the DORMOUSE,
the MOLE,
the HEDGEHOG,
the RACCOON,
the LIZARD,
the BAT,
and the OWL
cut the cake
into 9 *slices*.

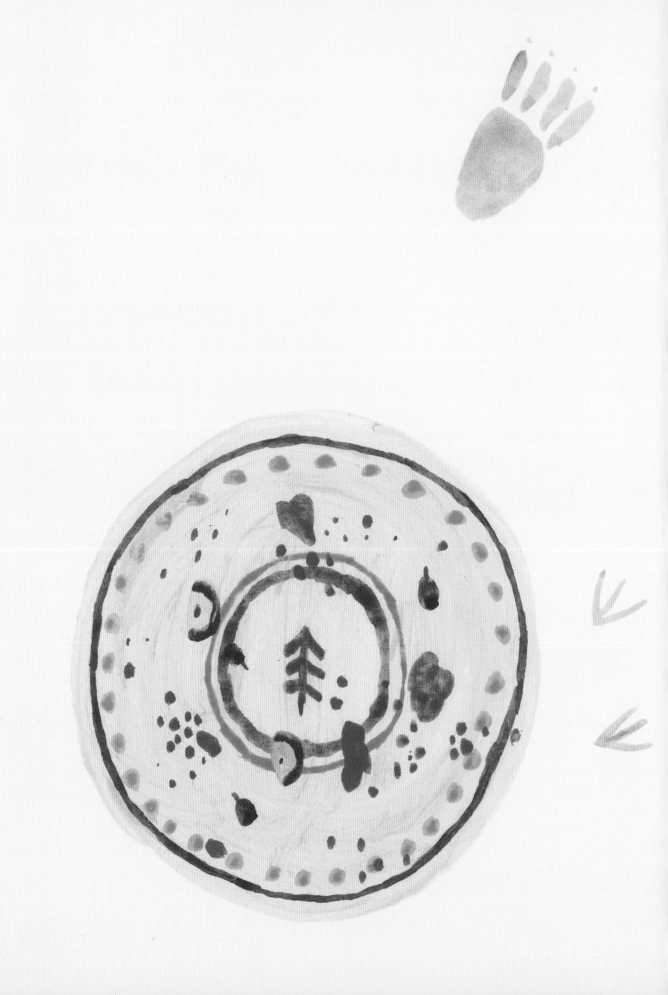

Which wasn't that hard
after all.

THE END

THE CAST

MOUSE *Idea*
BLACKBIRD *Flour*
DORMOUSE *Butter*
MOLE *Sugar*
HEDGEHOG *Apples*
RACCOON *Cinnamon*
LIZARD *Raisins*
BAT *Egg*
OWL *Oven*

Published by Princeton Architectural Press
A MCEVOY GROUP COMPANY
202 Warren Street, Hudson, New York 12534
www.papress.com

Good Morning, Neighbor text © 2017 Davide Cali
Illustrations © 2017 Maria Dek
Book design by Giulia Vetri
Published by arrangement with Debbie Bibo Agency

English edition © 2018 Princeton Architectural Press
All rights reserved. Printed and bound in China
by C&C Offset Printing Co., Ltd.
21 20 19 18 4 3 2 1 First edition

ISBN 978-1-61689-699-7

This book was illustrated using watercolors.

Princeton Architectural Press is a leading publisher
in architecture, design, photography, landscape,
and visual culture. We create fine books and stationery
of unsurpassed quality and production values. With
more than one thousand titles published, we find design
everywhere and in the most unlikely places.

For Princeton Architectural Press:
Editors: Amy Novesky and Nina Pick

Special thanks to: Ryan Alcazar, Janet Behning,
Nolan Boomer, Abby Bussel, Benjamin English,
Jan Cigliano Hartman, Susan Hershberg,
Kristen Hewitt, Lia Hunt, Valerie Kamen,
Jennifer Lippert, Sara McKay, Eliana Miller,
Wes Seeley, Sara Stemen, Marisa Tesoro,
Paul Wagner, and Joseph Weston of Princeton
Architectural Press —Kevin C. Lippert, publisher

Library of Congress Cataloging-in-Publication
Data available upon request.